Dear Parent:
Your child's love of reading starts here!

Every child learns to read in a different way and at his or her own speed. Some go back and forth between reading levels and read favorite books again and again. Others read through each level in order. You can help your young reader improve and become more confident by encouraging his or her own interests and abilities. From books your child reads with you to the first books he or she reads alone, there are I Can Read Books for every stage of reading:

SHARED READING
Basic language, word repetition, and whimsical illustrations, ideal for sharing with your emergent reader

BEGINNING READING
Short sentences, familiar words, and simple concepts for children eager to read on their own

READING WITH HELP
Engaging stories, longer sentences, and language play for developing readers

READING ALONE
Complex plots, challenging vocabulary, and high-interest topics for the independent reader

ADVANCED READING
Short paragraphs, chapters, and exciting themes for the perfect bridge to chapter books

I Can Read Books have introduced children to the joy of reading since 1957. Featuring award-winning authors and illustrators and a fabulous cast of beloved characters, I Can Read Books set the standard for beginning readers.

A lifetime of discovery begins with the magical words **"I Can Read!"**

Visit www.icanread.com for information
on enriching your child's reading experience.

I Can Read Book® is a trademark of HarperCollins Publishers.

Superman: I Am Superman
SUPERMAN and all related characters and elements are trademarks of DC Comics © 2010. All rights reserved.
Printed in the United States of America. No part of this book may be used or reproduced in any manner whatsoever without written permission except in the case of brief quotations embodied in critical articles and reviews. For information address HarperCollins Children's Books, a division of HarperCollins Publishers, 10 East 53rd Street, New York, NY 10022.
www.icanread.com

Library of Congress catalog card number: 2009933423
ISBN 978-0-06-187857-2
Typography by John Sazaklis

14 15 16 17 18 LP/WOR 20 19 18 17 16 15 ❖ First Edition

SUPERMAN™

I Am Superman

by Michael Teitelbaum
pictures by Rick Farley

SUPERMAN created by Jerry Siegel and Joe Shuster

HARPER
An Imprint of HarperCollinsPublishers

CLARK KENT

Clark Kent is a
newspaper reporter.
He is secretly Superman.

LOIS LANE

Lois Lane is a reporter.
She works for the
Daily Planet newspaper.

LEX LUTHOR

Lex Luthor is the
smartest criminal
in the world.
He is Superman's enemy.

THE FORTRESS OF SOLITUDE

This is Superman's
hidden home.
Many secrets about
his life are inside.

SUPERMAN

Superman has many amazing powers.
He was born on the planet Krypton.

Lois Lane sped past Clark Kent.

She was on her way out of

the Daily Planet,

where she and Clark worked.

They were newspaper reporters.

"Why are you in such a hurry, Lois?" asked Clark.

"I'm writing a story," Lois said.

"What kind of story?" Clark asked.

"That's my secret!" Lois said.

Lois rushed up to the roof.

Superman was waiting for her there.

"Hi, Lois," Superman said.

"Ready to do the story?"

"You bet, Superman!" Lois said.

"I thought we could talk somewhere
a little different," Superman said.

"Where are we going?" Lois asked.

"You'll see," said Superman.

Superman flew at super-speed
up to the frozen Arctic.

"This is my Fortress of Solitude,"
Superman said.

"The Fortress is my secret home,"

he told Lois.

"If you want to learn about me,

this is the best place to come."

"This giant key unlocks the door,"

Superman said.

He put the key into the lock.

"I use my super-strength to lift it."

Superman and Lois

entered the Fortress.

Superman used his super-breath

to blow the door closed.

"That's amazing!" said Lois.

Lois pointed at two statues.

"Who are those people?" she asked.

"Those are my parents,"

Superman said.

"My father, Jor-El,

and my mother, Lara.

They're holding a model of Krypton."

"Krypton?" Lois asked.

"Krypton was the planet
where I was born," Superman said.
"This crystal shows pictures
of life on Krypton."

"Krypton was different from Earth,
but it was my home," said Superman.
"Then one day my father learned
that Krypton was going to explode."

"My father put me in a spaceship
and sent it to Earth
to save my life," Superman said.

"Earth's yellow sun gives me
my superpowers," said Superman.
"Even when I was a little boy,
I could lift a truck."

"Wow," said Lois.

"What else can you do?"

"I can see through things

with my X-ray vision," Superman said.

"And nothing can hurt me."

"Nothing?" Lois asked.

"Only kryptonite can make me weak,"
Superman said.

"It's a piece of my home planet.

I keep it in this case so it can't hurt me."

Suddenly, an alarm rang out.

Lex Luthor's angry face

filled up the computer screen.

"I will rule the city!" said Luthor.

"Watch what will happen

if I'm not given complete power!"

"Metropolis is in danger!"
Superman said as he and Lois
zoomed out of the Fortress.
"I have to stop Luthor!"

Luthor blew up a building

as Superman and Lois arrived.

"The buildings are all empty,"

Superman said.

"At least no one got hurt."

"Metropolis is mine!"

said Luthor.

He blasted another building.

A piece of stone fell toward Lois.
Superman soared up to catch it
and then tossed it
safely away.

"I can destroy Luthor's laser
with my heat vision," Superman said.

Two red beams shot out of his eyes.

Luthor's weapon blew up.

Superman stopped Luthor's evil plot.

"Your days of making threats
are over!" he told the villain.

Superman gave Luthor to the police.

"Thanks for the story, Superman,"
Lois said when they returned to
the Daily Planet.

"I can't wait until Clark sees it!"

"Who's Clark?" Superman asked.

"Never mind!" Lois said.

The next day Lois hurried
into Clark's office.
She tossed a copy of
the Daily Planet onto his desk.

"Here's what I was doing
while you were just sitting around,"
Lois said to Clark.

"How do you do it?" Clark asked.

"That's my secret!" said Lois.

Lois walked out of Clark's office.

Clark smiled to himself.

"I have a secret, too," he said.

"I am Superman!"